IMAGINE THAT™

Licensed exclusively to Imagine That Publishing Ltd
Tide Mill Way, Woodbridge, Suffolk, IP12 1AP, UK
www.imaginethat.com
Copyright © 2022 Imagine That Group Ltd
All rights reserved
0 2 4 6 8 9 7 5 3 1
Manufactured in China

Written by Sam Samson
Illustrated by Vicky Lommatzsch

ISBN 978-1-80105-302-0

A catalogue record for this book is available from the British Library

Good Morning! Goodnight!

Written by
Sam Samson

Illustrated by
Vicky Lommatzsch

Early each morning, the zoo's daytime animals woke up. At that very moment, the night-time animals were getting ready for bed!

There was just enough time
for everyone to say, 'Good morning!' or,
'Goodnight!' And what a noise they all made!

THIS WAY

'Good morning!' squawked Parrot,
as loud as can be.

'Goodnight!' hooted Owl.
'It's bedtime for me!'

'Good morning!' screeched Monkey,
high up in the trees.

'Goodnight!' muttered Sloth.
'Now be quiet, please!'

LLAMA

'Good morning!'
mumbled Llama,
her mouth full of food!

'Goodnight!'
giggled Fox. 'That looks
terribly rude!'

'Good morning!'
snuffled Anteater, sniffing a mound.

'Goodnight!'
grunted Aardvark.
'I'll see you around.'

'Good morning!'
growled Bear,
her cub by her side.

EXIT

'Goodnight ...
I must fly!'
Sugar Glider replied.

'Good morning!' called Penguin, down by the pool.

'Goodnight!' answered Bat. 'I must hang somewhere cool.'

'Good morning!' said Giraffe.
'Now, which leaves are best?'

'Goodnight!' yawned Bushbaby,
snuggling up in her nest.

'Good morning!' snapped Crocodile,
with a big, toothy grin.

'Goodnight!' gulped Koala.
'It's time I turned in!'

'Good morning!' grinned Panda.
'It's another new day!'

RACCOON

KOALA

'Goodnight!'
answered Wombat.
'I'll sleep while you play!'

'Good morning!'
bellowed Elephant, taking a shower.

PANDA

'Goodnight!'
sighed Raccoon. 'I've been
up for hours!'

Finally, everyone enjoyed their
busy day, or their big sleep ...
until the moon appeared.

'Good morning!' called the night-time
animals, who were just waking up.

'Goodnight!' replied the daytime
animals, who were getting ready for bed.
And what a noise they all made!